DRAGON MASTERS

HOWL OF THE WIND DRAGON

BY

TRACEY WEST

BRANCHES

SCHOLASTIC INC.

DRAGON MASTERS

➤ Read All the Adventures ➤

More books coming soon!

TABLE OF CONTENTS

THANK YOU TO ALAN COVEY FOR PROVIDING

his expertise on the art and history of the Andes mountain range. — TW

Library of Congress Cataloging-in-Publication Data

Names: West, Tracey, 1965- author. | Howells, Graham, illustrator. | West, Tracey, 1965- Dragon Masters ; 20.
Title: Howl of the wind dragon / by Tracey West ; [illustrated by Graham Howells].
Description: First edition. | New York : Branches/Scholastic Inc., 2021. |
Series: Dragon Masters ; 20 | Summary: The wizard Astrid is planning to cast the False Life spell which will bring to life the bones of giant ancient beasts and allow her to conquer all the kingdoms; in order to prevent her the Dragon Masters must find the Wind Dragon, the final dragon needed to undo the spell—but that dragon and her Dragon Master are captives, and it is up to Drake and his friends to rescue them, and hope they are in time to stop Astrid.
Identifiers: LCCN 2020049483 (print) | LCCN 2020049484 (ebook) | ISBN 9781338635515 (paperback) | ISBN 9781338635522 (library binding) | ISBN 9781338635539 (ebook)
Subjects: LCSH: Dragons—Juvenile fiction. | Wizards—Juvenile fiction. | Magic—Juvenile fiction. | Rescues—Juvenile fiction. | Adventure stories. | CYAC: Dragons—Fiction. | Wizards—Fiction. | Magic—Fiction. | Rescues—Fiction. | Adventure and adventurers—Fiction. | LCGFT: Action and adventure fiction.
Classification: LCC PZ7.W51937 Hq 2021 (print) | LCC PZ7.W51937 (ebook) | DDC 813.54 [Fic]—dc23
LC record available at https://lccn.loc.gov/2020049483
LC ebook record available at https://lccn.loc.gov/2020049484

10 9 8 7 6 5 4 3 2 1   21 22 23 24 25

Printed in China   62

First edition, November 2021
Illustrated by Graham Howells
Edited by Katie Carella
Book design by Sarah Dvojack

FIND THE WIND DRAGON!

A flash of green light exploded in the Valley of Clouds behind King Roland's castle.

The light faded. Four Dragon Masters and their dragons appeared in the big, grassy field: Drake and his brown dragon, Worm. The Earth Dragon had transported them all there. Bo and his blue Water Dragon, Shu. Opeli and her Lava Dragon, Ka. And finally, Manawa and his Sea Dragon, Tani.

Tani was twice as big as any of the other dragons. Beautiful orange-and-yellow scales covered her body. Gills sprouted from each side of her enormous head.

Griffith the wizard, and Dragon Masters Ana and Rori, had been waiting in the valley. Rori's dragon, Vulcan, was with her. They all stared with wide eyes at Tani. They'd never seen her before.

"What a big dragon!" Rori cried.

"This is Tani, the Sea Dragon," Bo explained. "And Manawa is her Dragon Master."

Manawa bowed his head in greeting. "It is good to meet you all," he said. "We came here as quickly as we could."

"Yes, we want to help find the Wind Dragon!" Opeli added.

The Dragon Masters were in the middle of an important mission. An evil wizard named Astrid had taken over the Fortress of the Stone Dragon. She had turned Dragon Masters Mina and Caspar and their dragons into stone. And now she was about to cast a False Life spell. With that spell, she would bring to life the bones of giant ancient beasts. Then she could take them through magic portals to conquer kingdoms all over the world!

There was only one way to break the spell: with a Tenebrex Stone. But the Dragon Masters needed three dragons to make the stone's magic work. A Lava Dragon had to melt the stone. A Sea Dragon had to cool it. A Wind Dragon had to blow on it to transform it into a box. Then the box could break the spell.

Drake and his friends had found Ka and Tani. Now they needed one more dragon.

Ana stepped forward. "Rori and I found something," she said. "This book says there are Wind Dragons in a place called Ichu Mocco."

"They live in the mountains there," Rori added.

Griffith nodded at Rori. "You and Drake shall go find the Wind Dragon. The rest of us will stay here."

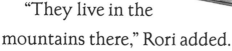

Rori pumped her fist in the air. "Yes! We'll find that Wind Dragon. Right, Vulcan?"

The Fire Dragon shot a small flame from his nose.

"Griffith, what happens *after* we find a Wind Dragon?" Drake asked.

"The three dragons will use their powers to transform the Tenebrex Stone," the wizard replied. "Then we will travel to the Fortress of the Stone Dragon. There are many wizards there already, trying to break down Astrid's defense spells so they can get inside. We'll need to be ready to battle, since Astrid will likely have an army of beasts by her side."

"We'll be ready," Drake promised.

Rori touched Drake with one hand and Vulcan with the other. "Let's go!" she cried.

Drake put a hand on his dragon. "Worm, take us to Ichu Mocco!"

CHAPTER 2

A WIND DRAGON!

Drake, Worm, Rori, and Vulcan transported in a flash of green. The light faded when they landed.

Drake blinked. A chilly breeze made him shiver. He looked around.

They stood on a stone platform on top of a mountain. Tall peaks rose up around them in every direction. The fluffy clouds in the sky looked close enough to touch.

We're very high up, he thought.

Dozens of small homes wound down the mountainside. But the biggest structure on the mountain sat on the very top: a tall stone wall surrounding a square courtyard. They had landed just outside the wall.

Warriors filled the courtyard. They wore brightly colored tunics, leather sandals, and drum-shaped hats. They faced a woman sitting on a stone throne. She wore

a dress and cloak with red, yellow, and orange designs. A band of silver circled her head.

She must be their queen, Drake guessed. And right next to her . . .

"That's a Wind Dragon!" Rori cried. "Just like the picture in the book."

Pale purple and white feathers covered the dragon's body and wings. She had long, slim ears and a face that reminded Drake of a horse.

"Look at the girl next to the dragon," Drake said. "Is she a Dragon Master?"

The girl had black braided hair that reached her waist. She wore a colorful skirt, and a red jacket over a white shirt. The sun glinted off a green gem hanging around her neck.

"Yes, she wears a Dragon Stone, just like we do," Rori said. "We need to talk to her!"

"Wait," Drake said. "There are a lot of warriors. They might attack when they see two dragons."

He looked at Worm, and his Dragon Stone glowed as the two of them connected. "Can you communicate with the Wind Dragon? We need to know if it's safe for us to approach."

Worm closed his eyes. His body glowed soft green.

Soon, Drake heard Worm's voice in his head.

I can sense the dragon's energy, but I can't get through to her. She is very upset. Something isn't right.

"Worm says something's wrong here," Drake told Rori.

"I know," Rori said. "Look!" She pointed to the dragon's leg.

Drake squinted to see. A thick silver chain bound the dragon to the queen's throne!

QUEEN AMARU

he Wind Dragon gazed at Drake, Worm, Rori, and Vulcan across the courtyard.

Drake thought her yellow eyes looked sad. "Dragons should never be chained up," he said.

Rori climbed on Vulcan's back. "We need to fly in there and free that poor dragon!"

"We have to do *something*," Drake agreed. "But we have to be careful. Those warriors have weapons. Rocks and slings."

Rori's eyes narrowed. "We can fight them!"

"We should try talking to their queen first," Drake said. "Worm can transport us right next to her throne. That will be safer than flying in over the warriors."

Rori frowned. "Fine." She climbed down.

Worm transported them to the throne.

The warriors pointed and shouted. The girl with the Wind Dragon stared at the Dragon Masters and their dragons.

"Silence!" the queen yelled, and the warriors settled down. She turned to Drake and Rori. "Do not dare try to attack with your dragons. We will destroy you!"

The queen's voice was loud and angry, and Drake trembled. Even Rori looked afraid.

Drake bowed. "We are not here to attack," he promised. "I am Drake, and this is my dragon, Worm. That's Rori and her dragon, Vulcan. We're from the Kingdom of Bracken, and we need your help."

"I am Queen Amaru," the ruler replied. She eyed Worm and Vulcan. "Why do you need my help when you have two strong dragons with you?"

Rori chimed in. "An evil wizard is casting a dangerous spell. We need your Wind Dragon to help stop her."

"We won't take long," Drake added.

Queen Amaru glared at them. "Do you think I am a fool? This is a plot to steal my dragon!"

"Your Highness, it's not a plot, we promise," Drake said. "The whole world could be in danger!"

"I'm afraid this is your problem, not mine," the queen replied. Then she gave Drake a snakelike smile. "But you are welcome to stay here with us. I would like to get to know your dragons better."

The way she said it gave Drake a chill.

"We don't have time for this!" Rori burst out. "If you would just —"

Drake grabbed Rori's sleeve. "Um, we just need to talk about it," he told the queen.

Queen Amaru frowned. "Be quick!"

Drake, Rori, Worm, and Vulcan moved away from the throne.

"That queen is bad," Rori whispered. "Drake, have Worm use his powers to free the Wind Dragon. Then we can all get out of here."

Drake looked at his dragon. "Will Rori's plan work?"

Before Worm could answer, loud screeching sounds filled the air. A flock of large black birds with white necks and pink wrinkled faces swooped down from the sky! They began to peck at the warriors!

The warriors swatted at the birds.

What is going on? Drake wondered, and then he heard a voice behind him.

"Please, Dragon Masters, can you help me?"

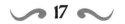

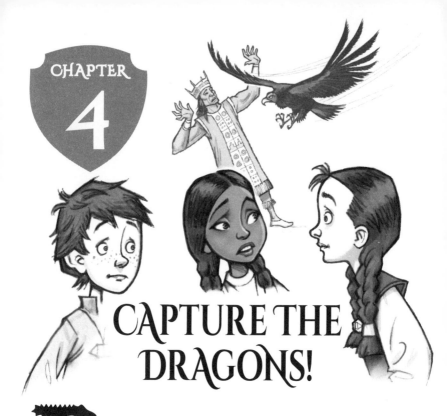

CHAPTER 4

CAPTURE THE DRAGONS!

The Wind Dragon's Dragon Master came up behind Drake and Rori.

"I am Quilla, and we don't have much time," the girl whispered, looking over her shoulder. "Wayra asked those birds to attack the warriors so I could talk to you."

"Wayra? Is that your dragon's name?" Rori asked.

Quilla nodded. "Yes. We need your help," she said. "Queen Amaru is very cruel. A few months ago, her warriors captured Wayra. The queen tried to control her, but Wayra wouldn't listen to her."

"Only a Dragon Master can communicate with a dragon," Drake said.

"Right. So then the queen's wizard found *me*," Quilla said. "Wayra and I already have a strong connection. But Queen Amaru doesn't know that. She wants me to ask Wayra to do bad things."

Rori frowned. "What kind of bad things?"

"She wants Wayra to use her powerful winds to destroy a village," Quilla replied. "But the people haven't done anything bad. Queen Amaru is just angry with them."

"Is that why you're pretending you don't have a connection with Wayra?" Drake asked.

"Yes," Quilla replied. "But I can't fake it much longer."

"Why can't Wayra use her wind powers to escape?" Rori asked.

"The chains are magical," Quilla explained. "Wayra can't use her wind powers when she is chained. She can't even fly."

Drake frowned. *A Wind Dragon needs to be able to sail and soar in the sky,* he thought.

"We'll help you both escape!" Rori cried.

The large birds screeched as they continued to attack the warriors.

"Wayra's distraction is working," Drake said. "Worm can magically transport us all to her. Then he can break —"

"Warriors! Ignore the birds. Those Dragon Masters are up to something. Capture their dragons!" Queen Amaru yelled, calling for the attack.

Six men charged toward the dragons.

Rori looked at Drake. "Free Wayra. Vulcan and I will keep the warriors busy."

Rori climbed on Vulcan's back. "Vulcan, fire!"
Vulcan shot a flaming fireball at the attackers.

The warriors jumped out of the way.

Drake, Quilla, and Worm hurried to the
Wind Dragon's side.

Queen Amaru shook her fists. "Warriors,
stop them!" she yelled.

"Worm, break those chains!" Drake cried,
pointing.

Worm glowed green.

Five men raced toward him. Rori and Vulcan zoomed down from the sky. Vulcan shot a stream of fire at the warriors.

They scattered.

The silver chains holding Wayra began to glow green. They trembled. Then they broke into tiny pieces!

Queen Amaru's face turned red. "Do not let my dragon get away!"

A third group of warriors charged at Wayra. She reared back — and howled!

ON THE MOUNTAIN

Aaaaaaaaooooooooooooooooooooooooooh!
A mighty wind blew from Wayra's mouth. It
glowed with pale purple energy.

Rori and Vulcan flew above the gale, escaping
its blast. But the force of the wind sent the warriors
sprawling backward.

Quilla jumped onto Wayra. "Drake, climb onto
Worm!" she yelled, over her dragon's howl.

27

"Worm can't fly!" Drake yelled back.

Quilla grinned. "He doesn't have to. Just hold on tight!"

Drake quickly obeyed.

Wayra's howl stopped for a moment. Then she howled again.

This time, the wind whipped around Wayra and Worm. It picked up the dragons and their riders and launched them into the air.

Down below, Queen Amaru shouted at them over the wind. "No one steals from Queen Amaru! I will find you. And your dragons will be mine!"

Drake had only flown on a dragon a few times before, and it always made him dizzy. He looked down as Wayra's magical wind swiftly carried them over the mountaintops. Fluffy clouds floated beneath them.

Rori and Vulcan flew up to meet them. "This is beautiful!" Rori cried. Her green eyes sparkled with excitement.

A few minutes later, Wayra gently set down on one of the mountains. Worm and Vulcan landed next to her.

Wayra says thank you, Worm told Drake as the Wind Dragon bowed her head at Drake and Rori.

"We're glad we could help," Drake said, and he climbed down from Worm. He saw only rocks and low-growing plants.

"Where are we?" he asked.

Before Quilla could answer, happy cries filled the air. Four Wind Dragons flew down from the clouds. They circled the Dragon Masters and their dragons.

Drake and Rori watched them, their mouths open in wonder.

"This is the Mountain of the Wind Dragons," Quilla explained. "Wayra is safe here. The queen's warriors can't reach her."

Rori frowned. "How did she get captured in the first place?"

Quilla looked at Wayra. "May I tell her?" she asked, and her dragon nodded.

"There was a storm," Quilla explained. "Wayra showed me images in my mind. Heavy winds and rains carried her away from this mountain. She crashed and got hurt, and the queen's warriors found her."

She smiled at her dragon. "But Wayra is better now."

Wayra smiled back. Then she lifted up in the air and joined her friends, flying joyfully in the sky.

"Quilla, we need to ask you a favor," Drake said. "Like we told Queen Amaru, we need Wayra's help."

"You shall have it!" Quilla replied. "Wayra and I would not be free if it weren't for you."

She whistled, and Wayra flew down to her.

"Wayra, we need to go on a journey with our new friends," Quilla told her dragon. "But we will return soon."

The Wind Dragon nodded. She flew back up to the other dragons.

"She is telling them she will be back," Quilla explained. "When do we leave?"

"Soon," Drake replied. He took out the magic mirror tucked into his belt.

"Griffith!" he said, and the face of the wizard appeared.

"Drake, have you found the Wind Dragon?" Griffith asked.

"Yes!" Drake replied.

"Good," Griffith said. "I need you all to transport to Belerion right away!"

THE GLOWING BONES

he wizard's face disappeared from the mirror.

"Belerion?" Rori asked. "Why is Griffith at the Castle of the Wizards?"

"We'll find out," Drake replied. He explained to Quilla and Wayra how Worm could use his powers to transport them there.

Then they all left the mountain, and arrived in Belerion in an instant.

They landed outside the castle, on the cliffs overlooking the sea. Quilla gazed up at the Castle of the Wizards. Its tall stone towers rose high in the sky. Jayana, the Head Wizard, and Griffith rushed toward them.

Griffith's eyes lit up when he saw Wayra. "A Wind Dragon! Well done," he said.

"This is Wayra, and her Dragon Master, Quilla," Rori said. "Where are Bo and Ana?"

"They're back in Bracken, guarding the castle," Griffith explained.

"You are just in time," Jayana said. "Astrid is casting the False Life spell."

"Is Astrid the evil wizard you were telling Queen Amaru about?" Quilla asked Drake.

"Yes," Drake replied.

The Head Wizard snapped her fingers and a small gazing ball appeared in her hand. She passed her palm over it. An image formed . . .

Astrid floated above the sand in the Garden of the Beasts. Giant bones all around her glowed with red magic. They were starting to shake and move.

The image faded.

"The bones are coming to life," Jayana said. "I will go to the fortress now to help the wizards break in. But you must transform the Tenebrex Stone and get to Navid as fast as you can! It's the only way we'll undo her terrible spell."

Jayana snapped her fingers again. *Poof!* She disappeared.

"Quickly! Follow me to the beach," Griffith told the Dragon Masters. "We will transform the stone there."

THE TENEBREX STONE

Griffith, Drake, Rori, Quilla, and the three dragons arrived on the beach. Opeli, Ka, and Manawa waited for them there. Tani floated in the sea. And Eko the Dragon Mage stood nearby with her Thunder Dragon, Neru.

Griffith opened the pouch he wore. He took out a white stone the size of a turnip, and perfectly round and smooth. He placed it in the sand.

"There are three steps to transform this stone," he began. "First, Ka must melt it."

Opeli nodded. "Ka, melt the Tenebrex!"

The Lava Dragon stomped up to the stone. His body glowed orange as lava rippled through it. Then he shot a stream of hot lava at the Tenebrex Stone. It bubbled as it began to melt.

"Now Tani must cool it with seawater," Griffith instructed.

"Tani, soak the stone!" Manawa cried.

The Sea Dragon aimed a blast of water at the stone. Steam rose from it as the Tenebrex Stone stopped melting. It cooled into a flat, rippled shape.

"Now the Wind Dragon must blow on it in order to transform it," Griffith instructed.

Quilla pointed at Wayra. "Use your wind power on the stone!"

Wayra blew on the stone. Her magical, pale purple wind swirled around it. The wind picked up the stone and swirled faster and faster. Bright sparks of purple light shot from the Tenebrex.

The wind died down. The transformed stone slowly floated back to the sand. It no longer looked like a white ball. Now it looked like a box swirling with purple, orange, and turquoise colors.

Griffith picked up the box and handed it to Drake. "I am trusting you with this, Drake," he said. "Keep it safe and be ready to use it!"

INTO THE FORTRESS

Drake stared at the beautiful box in his hands.

"How does this work?" he asked.

"Worm must get you as close as possible to the beasts. Then you'll unlatch the lid, open it, and the box will do the rest," Griffith replied.

Drake took the pouch from Griffith and tucked the box inside.

Eko approached. "Everyone must be ready to protect their lands, in case Astrid shows up with her beasts," she said. "Rori and Vulcan should return to Bracken. And I will take Opeli, Manawa, Quilla, and their dragons back to their kingdoms. Then I will join you at the fortress."

Quilla stepped forward. "It is not safe for Wayra and me to return to Queen Amaru," she said. "Please let us fight Astrid with you."

"Not safe?" Griffith asked.

"Queen Amaru had Wayra chained up," Drake explained. "She wanted her to do bad things. But Wayra has a safe home to go back to on the Mountain of the Wind Dragons."

"We will go there after we help you," Quilla said.

Griffith nodded. "Thank you. We could use the extra help. Now then, let's all get ready to go!"

Opeli and Manawa ran up to Drake and hugged him.

"Go stop that evil wizard!" Manawa said.

Opeli nodded. "I know you can do it."

"Thanks for all of your help," Drake replied.

Then Eko touched her purple dragon. "Neru, create a portal to our first stop: Kapua."

Neru let out a roar that sounded like thunder. Then a hole made of swirling purple energy appeared in the air.

"Step into it!" Eko instructed Opeli and Manawa.

The Dragon Masters and their dragons entered the portal. Eko and Neru followed them.

"I will see you in Navid!" Eko called out, and the portal closed.

Rori climbed onto Vulcan. "Good-bye, everyone! Quilla, you and your Wind Dragon are awesome!"

Quilla replied, "Thank you for your help!"

Rori and Vulcan flew off toward Bracken.

Drake turned to Quilla, Wayra, and Griffith. "Gather around Worm!" he cried.

Seconds later, they all landed outside the Fortress of the Stone Dragon. A line of soldiers stood at attention, along with a woman wearing a crown.

"Who are they?" Drake asked.

"I contacted Princess Daria of Navid," Griffith explained. "She and her soldiers are standing by in case Astrid attacks this land."

Jayana and dozens of other wizards stood between the soldiers and the fortress. Bright white magic streamed from the wizards' fingertips. It pushed against a band of red magic that circled the stone walls.

"Stand back," Griffith warned the Dragon Masters.

The white light grew brighter. Suddenly, it exploded! The wizards tumbled backward.

When the light faded, the red magic circle was gone. Astrid's defense spells had broken!

Jayana and some other wizards pointed at the heavy stone door blocking the entrance. It lit up with white magic and slid open.

"Find Astrid!" Jayana yelled, and the wizards rushed inside.

BONES OF THE BEASTS

Griffith, the two Dragon Masters, and their dragons followed the wizards into the fortress. Everyone stopped when they saw the stone statues: Mina of the Far North and Frost, her Ice Dragon. Caspar and his Stone Dragon, Shaka.

Quilla blinked. "Astrid did this?" she asked.

Drake nodded.

Jayana pointed to a group of wizards. "Stay here and free them from the stone."

Six wizards ran over to the statues.

"The rest of you will come with me," she instructed. "Astrid is with the bones. Drake, where can we find them?"

"Follow me," Drake replied, and he and Worm led the way.

They marched over to the entry to the Garden of the Beasts. A bright red light shone from inside. Drake shaded his eyes.

Through the light, he saw giant beasts —
beasts made of bones! Some beasts had a huge
body and a long, long neck. Others stood on two
feet, and had a huge head filled with sharp teeth!
Others had spiky spines, or a horn growing from
their forehead.

Another beast flew around the garden on
large wings. Its sharp, skinny beak looked like a
bird's beak.

Astrid floated above the sand. She wore a belt around her waist. Tiny, glowing bottles dangled from loops on the belt. Each one held a different color liquid — a dragon power she had stolen. If she drank one, she could use that dragon's attack as her own.

The evil wizard cackled loudly. "Come, my beautiful, bony beasts! Together, we will conquer the world!"

A swirling red portal opened up behind her.

Drake darted forward. "I have to use the Tenebrex Box!"

Griffith stopped him. "Wait, Drake! We need a plan to keep you safe."

"Wayra can help," Quilla piped up. "She can whip up a wind that will create a sandstorm around Astrid."

But Drake shook his head. "Astrid steals dragon powers. It's too dangerous."

"She won't see us coming!" Quilla promised. She climbed on Wayra's back. Her Dragon Stone glowed. "Wayra, create a sandstorm around that wizard!"

Just as Astrid stepped closer to the portal, Wayra lifted off the ground and flew into the Garden of the Beasts. The dragon's body glowed with soft purple magic, and the sand around Astrid whipped up. A spinning tornado of sand surrounded the wizard.

"Drake, now!" Griffith urged.

CHAPTER 10

LOST AND FOUND

The sand swirled around Astrid. The bone beasts stomped their feet and swung their necks, confused. Astrid was losing her control over them, thanks to Wayra's sandstorm.

Griffith said I have to get as close as possible to the beasts, Drake remembered, as he ran toward them. Then . . .

Boom! A blast of red magic burst through the tornado of sand. It knocked Drake off his feet. Wayra and Quilla spiraled across the garden.

"Wizards, blast Astrid with magic!" Jayana yelled, and a small army of wizards turned toward Astrid.

But the evil wizard quickly raised both hands in the air. The portal grew in size and began to suck the beasts inside it. Their shapes bent and twisted as they squeezed through the portal.

Astrid jumped through it last, just before the wizards could blast her.

Drake ran over to Quilla and Wayra. Quilla was on her feet, stroking her dragon's head.

"Is she okay?" Drake asked.

"Her right wing is hurt, but it's not serious," Quilla replied. "I am sorry Astrid got away."

"We tried our best. Her magic is really strong," Drake told his friend.

Griffith and Jayana rushed over.

"What do we do now?" Drake asked.

"I will use my magic on Astrid's portal to see where it leads," Jayana answered. "Then we'll follow her, and you must try to use the Tenebrex Box again."

"The last time we were here, Astrid said she wanted to attack the Land of the Far North," Drake said.

Griffith held up a magic mirror. "I will warn her sister, Hulda, that Astrid could be headed her way."

Then Drake remembered something. "Mina and Caspar!"

He ran to the courtyard. Quilla, Wayra, and Worm followed him to the stone statues of Mina, Caspar, and their dragons. Six wizards used wands to stream magic at the statues.

The statues began to tremble and crumble. Drake held his breath.

The stone dissolved into dust! In the statues' place stood Mina, Caspar, and their dragons, alive and well.

Mina shook the dust from her hair. "Astrid will pay for this!"

BEASTS, ATTACK!

Drake ran up to his friends and hugged them. "You're all right!" he cried.

"Yes," Mina said. "Now where is Astrid?"

"Is she still here, in the fortress?" Caspar added.

Drake shook his head. "No. She has brought the bones to life. Then she took the beasts with her through a portal and —"

"Drake was right! Astrid is in the Land of the Far North!" Jayana cried, running in with Griffith. "She's attacking King Albin's kingdom!"

Mina clenched her fist. "He is the king who banished her," she said. "Astrid is seeking revenge on him. And on her sister, Hulda, who is my wizard. We must go there right away!"

"Shaka and I will go, too," Caspar said. "It is our fault that Astrid was able to reach the bones."

As he spoke, Eko and Neru came through a purple portal.

"Opeli and Manawa are now safe in their kingdoms," Eko reported. "How else can I help?"

"You must take Quilla and Wayra back to the Mountain of the Wind Dragons," Griffith instructed. "Wayra is hurt, and must rest."

Quilla nodded. "I wish we could help you more, but Griffith is right," she said. She turned to Drake. "Thank you for helping us escape Queen Amaru. We will never forget you."

"We won't forget you two, either," Drake promised. "And we will stop Astrid!"

Eko, Neru, Quilla, and Wayra all stepped through a portal to Ichu Mocco.

"Everyone, to King Albin's castle!" Jayana cried. She snapped her fingers and vanished. The other wizards disappeared one by one.

"Before we go, we all need warmer clothes," Griffith said. He pointed at himself. *Poof!* Now he was dressed in warm, furry clothes. He did the same for the Dragon Masters.

Then Worm transported Drake, Griffith, Mina, Frost, Caspar, and Shaka to the Land of the Far North. They appeared outside the wall protecting King Albin's kingdom. The wizards were there, too, and Drake saw that Hulda had joined them. A thin layer of snow coated the ground.

Astrid stood in front of the massive wooden gate in the wall, surrounded by the beasts made of bones. The large, birdlike creature swooped overhead, making an eerie wailing sound.

Zap! Zap! Zap! Astrid attacked the wizards with powerful blasts of red magic.

Then she saw the Dragon Masters and their dragons.

"Beasts! Attack those three dragons!" she commanded.

CHAPTER 12

DRAGONS VS. BEASTS

The beasts all turned and faced the dragons. Worm began to glow green. Shaka stomped her massive feet. Frost flapped his wings.

"What should we do now?" Drake asked the others.

"We must go into battle!" Mina yelled.

"But if our dragons use their powers," Drake replied, "then Astrid will capture the powers and use them against us. You could be turned to stone again!"

"We wizards will keep Astrid busy," Griffith promised. "Drake, you and Worm must get as close as possible to the beasts and open the Tenebrex Box. Mina, Caspar, you must battle the beasts. They are only alive by magic, and they are just bones. Destroy them if you must."

"We will do what we have to!" Caspar cried.

Mina turned to Drake. "We'll try to force the beasts to group together," she told him. "When the time is right, have Worm teleport you into the middle of them."

Drake nodded. "Got it!"

Wizards surrounded Astrid, quickly trapping her in a magic bubble.

"Shaka, charge!" Caspar yelled.

The Stone Dragon charged toward some of the beasts. *Bam!* Shaka butted heads with a beast with a thick skull. The magical beast let out a strange, deep roar.

Mina and Frost flew toward a long-necked beast that towered over Frost.

"Frost, ice attack!" Mina cried.

Frost's body glowed with blue light. He shot icy breath at the giant beast.

The ice froze the creature's long neck. The bones shattered, and the beast crashed to the ground.

The crash startled the beasts nearby, and they pushed back toward the other group. On that side, a new beast ran toward Shaka, aiming to ram the Stone Dragon with a sharp horn.

Smash! The powerful Stone Dragon stomped on the ground, making it shake. The beast fell on its side, and the bones landed in a messy pile.

Then Mina and Frost flew overhead. They circled the beasts, drawing them closer together.

Drake glanced at Astrid. The wizards still had her suspended in the magic bubble.

Mina flew past Drake. "Use the box now!"

Drake thought quickly. "Worm, transport us closer to the beasts!"

In a flash of green light, they landed in the center of the creatures. A long, bony tail thrashed at Drake and he jumped to the side.

He heard Worm's voice in his head. *I can freeze the ones closest to you.*

Drake knew what that meant. Worm didn't freeze things by making them cold, like Frost did. He froze them with his mind, and they stopped moving.

Worm's body glowed. The beasts around Drake froze.

He took the Tenebrex Box out of his pouch and set it down on the snow. Then he reached for the latch on the lid...

Boom! Before he could open it, a blast of red magic rocked the Land of the Far North. Drake fell backward, away from the box.

Astrid burst through the wizards' magic bubble. She floated in the air over to the box.

"You will not stop me!" she yelled, reaching for the magical box.

THE MAGIC OF THE TENEBREX

N**o!" Drake cried, lunging for the Tenebrex Box.

Suddenly, Mina swooped down on Frost and yanked the belt off Astrid's waist. The glass bottles clanked together. Astrid landed on the ground.

"Give that back!" Astrid shrieked, reaching for the belt in Mina's hands. Her fingers grazed the bottles.

Shaka stomped up to Astrid, roaring.

"Shaka, make a pit!" Caspar cried.

Shaka stomped, and a huge hole opened up in the frozen ground.

Drake pushed Astrid into it.

"Frost, ice!" Mina yelled as they flew past the pit.

The Ice Dragon breathed, and a thick layer of ice covered the pit. Through the ice, Drake could hear the evil wizard's muffled, angry screams: "This ice will not hold me!"

Griffith, Jayana, Hulda, and the other wizards quickly surrounded the pit.

Now, Drake! Worm told him.

Drake opened the lid of the Tenebrex Box. Streams of purple, orange, and turquoise magic shot out, lighting up the sky. The lights snaked out across the snowy land, wrapping around the beasts.

First, the beasts stopped moving. Then the bones clattered to the ground and landed in piles all over the snow.

The lights faded. Then the box transformed back into an orb-shaped stone. Drake picked it up and put it back into the pouch.

Mina and Frost landed next to Drake. "You did it!" Mina cried.

Drake gazed around at the lifeless bones. "Yes, we all did it," he said. "The False Life spell has been broken. And Astrid is trap —"

Whoosh! A beam of bright white light shot through the icy pit holding the wizard! The light melted all of the ice!

A SISTER'S PLEA

strid floated up out of the pit, and light streamed from her mouth! She held an empty bottle in her hand.

She must have grabbed a bottle of dragon powers when she was struggling with Mina, Drake guessed. *But I've never seen a power like that! She's unstoppable! Unless ... it's a risk, but there's no choice now.*

"Worm, freeze Astrid!" Drake yelled.

Worm's body glowed green again, and Astrid stopped moving in midair. The light stopped streaming from her mouth.

Her magic is very strong, Worm told Drake. *I can't hold her for long.*

"Worm needs some help!" Drake yelled, and all the wizards stepped forward. They pointed at Astrid and surrounded her in another magic bubble.

Hulda pleaded with her sister. "Astrid, it doesn't have to be this way. I know you are angry with King Albin. But revenge will not solve anything. Surrender to us. End this now."

Astrid looked frozen in the bubble. But then her eyes glowed red, the color of dark magic. Her mouth began to move.

She's resisting the powers of Worm and the wizards! Drake realized.

"Do you think I can be beaten so easily?" Astrid asked. "After I take King Albin's kingdom, I will grow stronger. I will keep defeating lands until I rule the world!"

She cackled with evil laughter. Then the magic bubble burst! A swirling portal opened up in the air. Worm's energy still held her, but she managed to reach toward the portal.

"She's going to escape!" Mina cried.

Caspar stepped forward. "She won't get away this time! Shaka, use your secret power — turn her to stone!"

84

A VISITOR

Two gray beams of light shot from Shaka's eyes as Astrid moved closer to the portal. The dragon's power beams hit her. Instantly, the wizard's body turned to stone.

Everyone was silent for a moment. Shaka's body stopped glowing. Worm gently lowered the statue to the ground.

Hulda walked up to her sister and touched her face. "Astrid is . . . a statue," Hulda said.

Mina joined Hulda. "I am sorry that I could not stop her from reaching the beasts in the first place." She looked down at the snow.

Hulda patted Mina's arm. "My sister was too powerful for her own good. No one could stop her alone. It took all of us working together to do it. And I know King Albin will be relieved that Astrid is no longer a threat to him and his people."

"Can she break through the stone with her magic?" Caspar wondered.

"She should not be able to escape," Jayana said. "But we will bring her to the Wizard's Council prison to make sure."

"What happens now?" Drake asked, handing the pouch with the Tenebrex Stone back to Griffith.

"Now you shall all go home and rest," Griffith said.

"I could use a warm bath and some onion stew," Drake admitted.

Griffith turned to Jayana. "I will help you take Astrid to the prison. Can one of your wizards help get Caspar and Shaka back to Navid?"

Jayana nodded. "I'll take care of it."

Drake hugged Mina and Caspar good-bye.

"Drake, you will always have a friend in Navid," Caspar said.

"You are more than my friend now, Drake," Mina said. "You are my brother."

Drake smiled. "I've always wanted a sister."

Griffith magically returned their clothes to the way they were before. *Poof!*

Then Drake touched his dragon. "Let's go home now, Worm."

The dragon transported them to Bracken, to the Valley of Clouds outside the castle.

Drake yawned. "It's warm and sunny here," he said. "How about a nap?"

That sounds nice, Worm replied.

Drake slid down and rested against Worm's back. He closed his eyes.

A few minutes later, he felt something on his arm. He looked down, expecting to see a field snake, or maybe a toad. He blinked.

A tiny dragon crawled on him. It wasn't much bigger than his foot. Green scales covered the dragon's body, and white flower petals sprouted from the dragon's head. The dragon's wings looked like flower petals, too.

Drake sat up. His eyes got wide. "Worm, we have a visitor!"

TRACEY WEST has often wondered, "What would a battle between dinosaurs and dragons look like?" She wrote this book to answer that question.

Tracey is the author of the *New York Times*-bestselling Dragon Masters series; the Pixie Tricks series; and dozens more books for kids. She shares her home with her husband, her dogs, and a bunch of chickens. They live in the misty mountains of New York State, where it is easy to imagine dragons roaming free in the green hills.

GRAHAM HOWELLS lives with his wife and two sons in west Wales, a place full of castles and legends of wizards and dragons.

There are many stories about the dragons of Wales. One story tells of a large, legless dragon — sort of like Worm! Graham's home is also near where Merlin the great wizard is said to lie asleep in a crystal cave.

Graham has illustrated several books. He has created artwork for film, television, and board games, too. Graham also writes stories for children. In 2009, he won the Tir Na N'Og award for *Merlin's Magical Creatures*.

DRAGON MASTERS
HOWL OF THE WIND DRAGON

Questions and Activities

Quilla wants to keep her connection to Wayra a secret from Queen Amaru. Why? Reread pages 19–20.

Astrid can travel through portals to attack any kingdom. So most of the Dragon Masters return home to protect their lands. Why does Quilla stay with Drake?

Astrid takes her army of beasts to the Land of the Far North. Why does she want to attack this kingdom first? Turn back to page 64. (*Psst!* If you have *Fortress of the Stone Dragon*, reread pages 4–7 in that book!)

Caspar commands Shaka to turn Astrid into stone. Do you think he makes the right choice? Why or why not?

In this book, Drake and Worm travel to five different locations. List them all. Then draw the one where you would most want to live!